ELMHURST PUBLIC LIBRARY
3 1135 02156 6549
W9-CAZ-359

Dear Parents and Educators,

Welcome to Penguin Young Readers! As parents and educators, you know that each child develops at their own pace—in terms of speech, critical thinking, and, of course, reading. Penguin Young Readers recognizes this fact. As a result, each Penguin Young Readers book is assigned a traditional easy-to-read level (1–4) as well as an F&P Text Level (A–P). Both of these systems will help you choose the right book for your child. Please refer to the back of each book for specific leveling information. Penguin Young Readers features esteemed authors and illustrators, stories about favorite characters, fascinating nonfiction, and more!

Dirt and Bugsy: Bug Catchers

LEVEL 2

F&P TEXT LEVEL I

This book is perfect for a **Progressing Reader** who:

- can figure out unknown words by using picture and context clues;
- can recognize beginning, middle, and ending sounds;
- can make and confirm predictions about what will happen in the text; and
- can distinguish between fiction and nonfiction.

Here are some **activities** you can do during and after reading this book:

- Make Connections: Dirt and Bugsy love to find and play with bugs. What kind of animals do you like to play with? Do you like to collect and sort anything the same way Dirt and Bugsy do?
- Problem/Solution: In this story, it begins to rain on the bugs that Dirt and Bugsy have collected. What solution do they come up with to solve this problem?

Remember, sharing the love of reading with a child is the best gift you can give!

*This book has been officially leveled by using the F&P Text Level Gradient™ leveling system.

For Brendan and Connor, whose brains are always buzzing with good ideas—ML

Mom, Dad, and Shayla, thank you for your constant support, love, and encouragement. To my agent, Chad, thank you for believing in me and having my back—SLP

PENGUIN YOUNG READERS
An imprint of Penguin Random House LLC, New York

First published in the United States of America by Penguin Young Readers, an imprint of Penguin Random House LLC, New York, 2023

Visit us online at penguinrandomhouse.com.

Library of Congress Cataloging-in-Publication Data is available.

Manufactured in China

ISBN 9780593519912 (pbk) 10 9 8 7 6 5 4 3 2 1 WKT
ISBN 9780593519929 (hc) 10 9 8 7 6 5 4 3 2 WKT

PENGUIN YOUNG READERS

LEVEL 2 PROGRESSING READER

Dirt and Bugsy

Bug Catchers

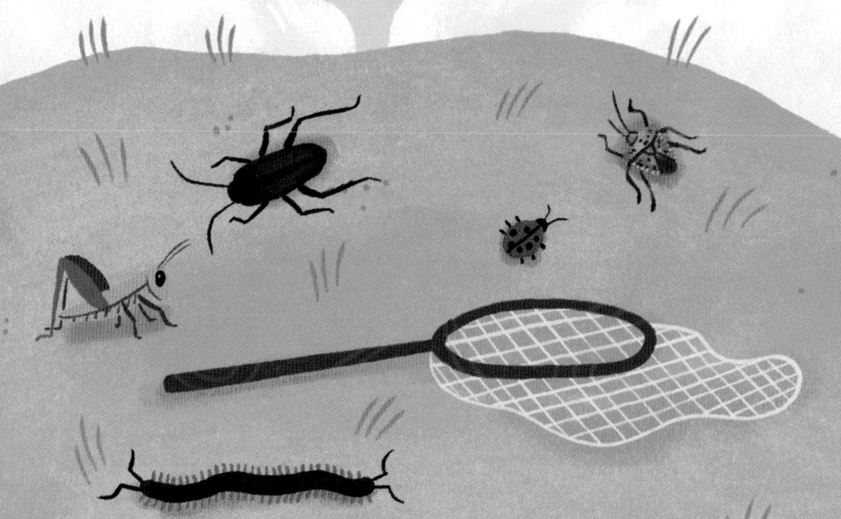

by Megan Litwin

illustrated by Shauna Lynn Panczyszyn

Dirt and Bugsy are bug catchers.

They catch all kinds of bugs.

Bugs that crawl.

Bugs that fly.

Bugs that slide.

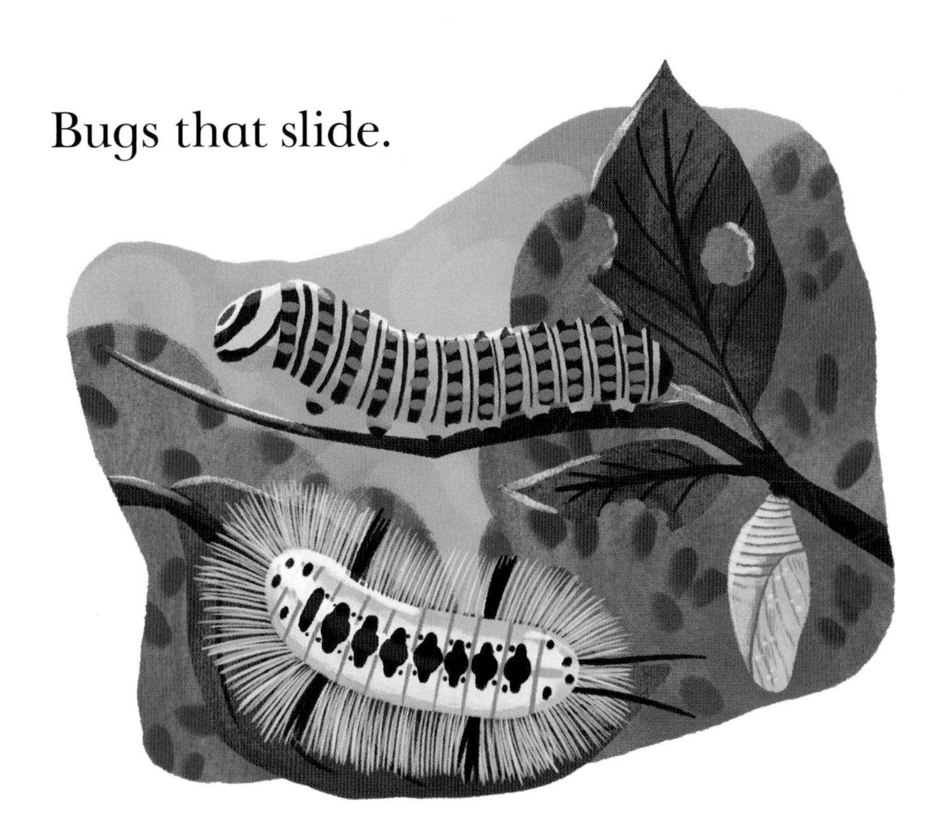

Bugs that hide.

Every day the bug boys set out.

Dirt with his shovel.

Bugsy with his jars.

They spy.

They dig.

They lift.

They sift.

It is afternoon.

Dirt and Bugsy are outside.

Bugs are crawling up, down,

all around.

Up arms.

Down legs.

All around the ground.

Dirt and Bugsy don't mind.

They love bugs!

But then it starts to rain.

Dirt and Bugsy are getting wet.

The bugs are getting wet, too.

The bug boys think.

Their brains buzz.

They come up with a plan.

They will build a shelter.

They will build the very best one.

They will build . . . a bug barn!

ALL BUGS WELCOME
OPEN

Bugsy runs to
find more jars.

Dirt runs to
dig up more dirt.

They get grass and twigs.

They get rocks and sand.

They make big rooms and
small rooms and rooms in between.
And soon, they have a bug barn.

But now—they have no bugs.

Not to worry.

Dirt and Bugsy are good bug catchers.

They spy.

They dig.

They lift.

They sift.

They catch all kinds of
bugs in no time at all.

They give each bug a room.

They give each bug some food.

They give each bug a name.

Then they all play some games.

And when the rain has stopped,
the bugs go home.

Some crawl.

Some fly.

Some slide.

Some hide.

"Goodbye, goodbye," Bugsy calls after them.

"Catch you later," says Dirt.

And they will.

Dirt and Bugsy are good bug catchers.
They catch all kinds of bugs.

Again, and again, and again . . .

HOW TO BE A GOOD BUG CATCHER

1. Find a good bug-catching jar.

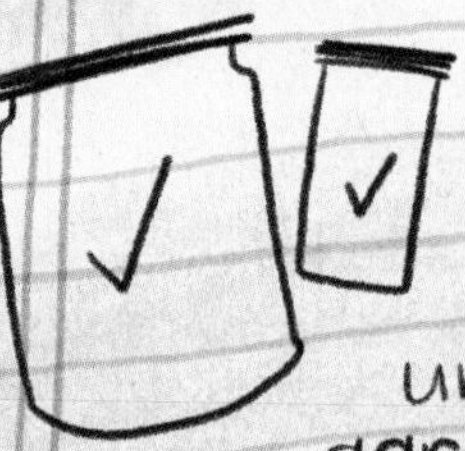

2. Go outside. Look around in good buggy places like: under rocks, under logs, on flowers, in gardens, on trees, and near lights.

3. Put the bug inside the jar.

4. Give it food, water, and air.

5. Watch it. Name it. Draw it. Have fun with it!

6. Set it free and let it be.

7. Catch a new bug.